THE LONG-LOST SECRET DIARY OF THE WORLD'S WORST KNIGHT

Book design by David Salariya
Illustrations by Sarah Horne
Additional cover illustrations by Tanya Komedina

Published in the United States by Jolly Fish Press, an imprint of North
Star Editions, Inc.

First US Edition
First US Printing, 2018

This is a work of fiction. Names, characters, places, and incidents are
either the product of the author's imagination or are used fictitiously, and
any resemblance to actual persons living or dead, business establishments,
events, or locales is entirely coincidental.

Library of Congress Cataloging-in-Publication Data (pending)
978-1-63163-137-5 (paperback)
978-1-63163-136-8 (hardcover)

Jolly Fish Press
North Star Editions, Inc.
2297 Waters Drive
Mendota Heights, MN 55120
www.jollyfishpress.com

Printed in the United States of America

THE LONG-LOST SECRET DIARY OF THE WORLD'S WORST KNIGHT

Written by
Tim Collins

Illustrated by
Sarah Horne

JOLLY
FiSH
PRESS
Mendota Heights, Minnesota

Chapter I
— ⊢—⊣ —
Knight Training

February Ist

Step aside, Sir Lancelot. Make way, Sir
Gawain. Nice try, Sir Galahad.

Forget all the heroic knights you know. This is
the tale of the bravest and wisest knight of all–
Sir Roderick. Me!

Okay, maybe that's not true.

I'm not even a knight yet. I'm still a squire to Sir Lionel here at Doddingford Castle, and I won't be made a knight for at least another three years.

And I'm not entirely brave. But I can be wise on a good day. One out of three isn't bad.

But soon I will be brave, and I know I'll make a brilliant knight.

This secret diary will record how I rose to greatness. One day they'll tell stories about me, just as they do about King Arthur and the Knights of the Round Table and Roland and all the others.

The difference is that all the details of my life will be written down here, so people in the future will know exactly what I did.

8

February 2nd

Sir Lionel set me a very important challenge today. I had to clean all the pigeon poo off the east wall of the castle. The stain was really high up, and I had to go all the way to the top of the ladder to get it off.

That was pretty brave, right?

It might not have been as brave as galloping fearlessly toward an enemy with my visor down and my lance raised. But it's an important step. Today, wiping away pigeon poo. Tomorrow, wiping out the enemy on the field of battle.

And today's job did turn out to be quite a perilous quest, because I wore my fashionable pointed shoes and ended up falling off the ladder.

I was so brave I didn't even cry when I hit the ground. Well, not that much.

February 3ʳᵈ

Sir Lionel gave me another brilliant quest today. I had to wash all his flags. The water was really cold, and it was very brave of me to dip my hands all the way in and . . .

Who am I kidding?

Washing the flags was just another boring job. They weren't even that dirty.

As I cleaned the flags in the corner of the courtyard, I spotted Thomas and Geoffrey practicing their sword skills on a wooden post.

Thomas is the squire to Sir Hugh and Geoffrey is the squire to Sir Robert. Their lords obviously believe they're capable of learning better stuff. So why doesn't mine?

GET REAL

Before someone became a knight he had to train for a few years as a squire. He'd learn to fight and act as a personal assistant to an existing knight, looking after the knight's weapons and armor.

February 4th

Brilliant news—today I asked Sir Lionel if he could train me in sword fighting and he agreed. I think it helped that Sir Hugh and Sir Robert were with him. Even if he doesn't think I'm ready yet, he'd never admit it in front of those two. The knights all get really competitive about who has the best sword, or lance, or coat-of-arms. It stands to reason they're also competitive about who has the best squire.

I'm getting my first lesson tomorrow. I had to spend today cleaning cups and plates for the upcoming feast, but I didn't mind. My new life as a mighty warrior begins tomorrow, and I'll never have to bother with boring chores again.

I'm writing this on my pile of straw in the corner of the Great Hall, where all us squires sleep. I have a really cozy spot just along the wall from the fire, and I've managed to gather loads of really soft straw. I usually have no problem drifting off to sleep, but I'm too excited tonight.

I just want it to be tomorrow so I can start my new life.

February 5ᵗʰ

It turns out sword stuff is a lot harder than it looks. Sir Lionel led me out to the wooden post this morning and handed me a sword that was almost as big as me. He said practicing with weapons that were too big would help build my muscles. It won't be long before I'm trotting off on quests and fighting people for real, so I need to be as strong as I can be.

I tried to lug the sword up and strike the post. The tip stayed on the ground.

I told my arms to lift the sword, but they ignored me. I bent my knees, then thrust myself up while swinging my arms around.

This time it worked. I spun round and round until the sword was over my head.

This was it! I was becoming a merciless warrior.

The courtyard was turning into a dizzy blur. A small part of my mind wondered why I hadn't struck the wooden post yet, but I was so giddy about my new skill I ignored it.

A few seconds later I struck what I thought was the post. But when the world stopped revolving I saw I'd actually circled all the way across the courtyard and sunk the sword into the side of a spinning wheel.

All around me, people were crouching in

14

corners and cowering behind their hands.
So the good news is that I struck fear into
people with my sword skills. The bad news is
they weren't my enemies and I didn't mean
to strike fear into them. But if I can make the
right people feel that frightened, I'll be well on
my way to becoming an amazing knight.

February 6th

Sir Lionel said we should give the sword

fighting a rest and focus on other training activities. He took me to a field at the back of the castle, close to the North Hills. We were out of sight of the others, which meant I could focus on my training without worrying about anyone watching.

First, I tried fighting with a long wooden stick called a quarterstaff. Sir Lionel showed me how to lunge it forward to repel lance and sword attacks. I think I was concentrating on the top too much, because the bottom swung round and took my feet out.

Looking at it in a positive way, I used the element of surprise, which is important in battle. It's just a shame I used it on myself and not an enemy.

Next, we tried putting the stone. In this exercise, you have to throw a huge rock as

far as you can. I got it quite high, but sadly not very far. The rock plummeted down onto my foot, and I hopped about and screamed. I launched a deadly attack on myself. Again.

Finally, we tried acrobatics training. I had to tip forward, support my weight with my hands, and hold my legs in the air. I could manage this quite easily, if Sir Lionel held my legs up. So maybe I didn't do too brilliantly on my training today either. But it's difficult to learn three new things in one day! Give me a week and I'll be an expert in all this stuff.

GET REAL

A squire's training would include lots of different activities to help improve his fitness and skill. Activities included wrestling and acrobatics, as well as training with weapons such as swords, javelins, and quarterstaffs.

February 7th

When I asked Sir Lionel what I'd be doing today, he pointed to a pile of cups in the corner of the courtyard. Looks like I'm back to the chores again.

Bah. I get two measly attempts at knight training, and I'm put right back on the boring jobs. And all because my training attempts didn't go as well as they might have.

I had to watch Thomas and Geoffrey practicing their sword skills while I washed the cups. I bet they weren't perfect at first either. The difference is they had patient masters who didn't give up on them after their first tiny mistake.

Chapter 2
—
A Visit from Sir Reginald

February 8th

Okay. Maybe things aren't so bad. I asked Sir Lionel when I could go back to battle training, and he said he'd consider it next week. For now, I've got to wash all the plates and cups for the feast tomorrow. A knight called Sir Reginald is coming to visit, and they're putting on a banquet in his honor. Because he's such an important guest, he's staying in the bedroom at the top of the keep, and we're going to serve him our best food.

Sir Reginald sounds like an amazing knight, and I expect just seeing him will be a real inspiration. No doubt I'll be totally fired up when I return to my training.

February 9th

Sir Reginald arrived at the castle this morning, and the knights have been scoffing constantly

ever since. They've eaten beef, mutton, swan,
and peacock. I served pheasant to Sir Reginald,
and he got angry with me because I didn't carve
it properly. Apparently that's another skill Sir
Lionel is meant to have taught me. Perhaps
Sir Reginald should take that up with him.

Sir Reginald is an overweight and red-faced man who isn't much taller than me. He looks like he'd keel over and die if he tried to pick up anything bigger than a table knife. I did actually find him quite inspiring, though. If he can become a great knight, there's hope for me.

When he wasn't getting annoyed with me for not carving the meat properly, he was getting angry about the knights of Froddington Castle. They recently stole the fingers of Saint Stephen, which is an important holy relic, from Yellowfriars Monastery.

This news sent our knights into a rage, and soon they were all as red and cross as Sir Reginald. Our jester Leofric came in to entertain them, but they threw bones and vegetables at him. Most people usually wait until he starts telling jokes for that.

He really needs to learn to pick his moments.
He's always telling me timing is important
for comedy. And yet he wanders into a room of
knights who've worked themselves into a frenzy
over some missing fingers and expects them to
want to laugh.

GET REAL

Lavish banquets were often thrown in medieval times to impress guests. Rich and exotic foods would be served, and diners would be entertained by musicians, acrobats, and jesters. Squires would sometimes be called upon to carve the meat for their masters.

February 10th

I was expecting my job today to be cleaning up after the feast, and I wasn't looking forward to it. But this morning Sir Lionel said that I had to attend to Sir Reginald instead. Apparently he'd been struck down by a mysterious illness, and I had to watch over him in case his condition got worse.

His illness didn't seem very mysterious to me. He spent the whole of yesterday eating, and he spent today lying in bed and clutching his stomach.

Every so often he'd throw up into his bucket, and I'd have to chuck it out the window.

He was constantly retching and whimpering, but at least that meant he couldn't complain I wasn't throwing the vomit away properly.

At one point I opened the window to toss out the latest helping of spew, and bright sunlight streamed in. Sir Reginald bolted upright in bed and shouted, "Yes, yes, I see!"

He stared at me with his hand out, then collapsed back down to the bed. At first I thought he'd died, and I was worried everyone would blame me for not looking after him properly. But when I leaned in close to listen to his heartbeat, a fresh fountain of spew erupted from his mouth and went all over my hair.

I don't think I can take another day of this. I never thought I'd say it, but I really hope I can go back to cleaning dishes tomorrow.

*February II*th

Today was the greatest day of my life. I would never have imagined that cleaning up vomit could lead to such amazing fortune.

This morning, Sir Lionel told me that Sir Reginald had miraculously recovered from his illness, and I could go back to cleaning up plates. I was just getting started when he called me into the great hall. Apparently, Sir Reginald had called all the other knights for a meeting, and he'd personally asked that I go too. I hoped it wasn't because he thought he might still have a bit of vomit left and he needed someone to scoop it up.

When everyone was settled in the hall, he announced his news. While he was stricken with illness, he'd been given a vision by Saint Stephen. The Saint had told him to go on a quest to get his fingers back from the evil Froddington knights and return them to Yellowfriars Monastery.

Saint Stephen had declared there should be twelve knights on the quest, to match the number of Knights of the Round Table.

There were murmurs of confusion from the others. There are only ten knights here at the castle, so even if we added Sir Reginald we'd still be one short.

And that's when the brilliant bit happened. Apparently, Saint Stephen had given Sir Reginald a vision of me with holy light shining behind me, meaning I should become the extra knight for their quest.

I was about to admit it wasn't a vision at all, and that I was actually standing in his room with the sun behind me after throwing his vomit out, but thank goodness I kept my mouth

BLEUGH!

shut. I know knights are meant to be honest, but there are moments when it pays to bend the truth a little.

It took a few moments for Sir Reginald's words to sink in. He was talking about making me a knight right away. This would cut out years of training and waiting, and it would definitely mean no more washing dishes and cleaning up pigeon poo. I'd be going straight from zero to hero.

Sir Robert and Sir Hugh tried to spoil things by saying I wasn't ready, and if we were desperate for another knight, Thomas or Geoffrey would be more suitable.

I tried to think of a way to argue back, but I couldn't. Both Thomas and Geoffrey are pretty handy with their swords, and it would be much

better to have one of them in a crisis than let me loose to attack my own feet. But I really wanted to become an awesome knight, and that must count for something.

It turned out that I didn't have to justify myself. Sir Reginald shouted at them until he was purple for doubting Saint Stephen. He said he'd refuse to stand for anyone questioning a vision personally given to him by a saint.

So that was it. It was agreed that I should be made a knight right away.

Sir Lionel even looked quite proud of me for once. He grinned at Sir Robert and Sir Hugh as they folded their arms and scowled.

Our quest begins on the first day of next month, by which time the worst of the winter weather

should be over. It will also give them time to knight me, train me properly, and hold a tournament in my honor.

Yeah, you read that last bit right. They're putting on an entire tournament to celebrate my brilliantness. Eat my dust, losers.

GET REAL

The legend of King Arthur and the Knights of the Round Table was incredibly popular in the Middle Ages. According to the stories, the knights lived in a castle called Camelot and went on quests to find the Holy Grail, the cup that Jesus, according to Christian tradition, drank from at the last supper. No one is sure if King Arthur even existed, but the myths about him were an inspiration to real knights.

Chapter 3

⊢—⊣

I Become
a Knight

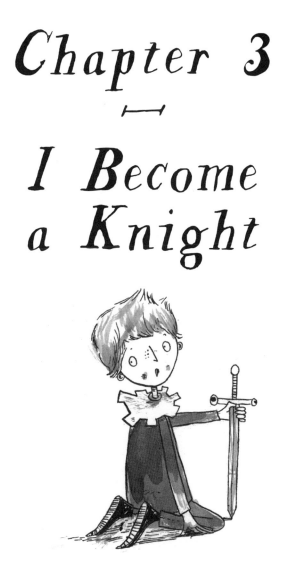

February 12th

Sir Lionel took me to the armory this morning
to choose a sword. I'm not usually allowed
in, although I've sneaked inside a few times
at night.

Stepping inside without having to worry
about getting caught was amazing. I stood in
the middle of the murky space, surrounded
by suits of armor, longbows, arrows, spears,
maces, lances, axes, daggers, and staffs. It
was finally sinking in. I was going to become a
real-life hero.

We headed for the back wall, where swords
were hanging from a long wooden rack.

Sir Lionel told me to pick the sword that
was calling out to me. My eyes fixed on a
huge silver one with a copper crossguard.

I pointed at it, and Sir Lionel said I'd made an excellent choice. He said it was double-edged and powerful enough to tear links of chain mail apart.

I tried to grab the sword, but it wouldn't budge. I put both my hands on the grip, and I tried again. I still had no luck.

It was a bit like the story of the sword in the stone, if King Arthur had totally failed to pull the sword out of the stone.

Sir Lionel pointed to the sword beneath it. He said it was almost as big but had a groove running down the middle of the blade that made it much lighter.

This one I managed to pull out. I held it in the air and imagined my enemies cowering in fright.

I found myself stumbling backward. My knees were weak, and my arm was quaking. My imaginary enemies were sniggering at me now. This wasn't good. I couldn't even frighten a pretend foe.

Sir Lionel grabbed the sword, stuck it back in the rack, and picked out a small pointed one. It was very thin and wasn't even half the length of the others, but I could hold it without collapsing.

So that's my sword. It's not the most impressive one ever seen, but I still expect it to be claiming the lives of bad guys very shortly.

This evening Sir Reginald came to my room and told me all about the tournament they're planning. He's invited a group of knights from nearby Bamwell Castle to compete at jousting with us.

He says he's counting on me to win all my bouts and show the Bamwell lot why he knighted me.

Er . . . he knighted me because he ate too much meat and thought Saint Stephen told him to. But never mind. I'm sure I'll be good at jousting. All you have to do is knock your opponent off his horse with a stick. How hard can that be?

GET REAL

According to myth, Arthur revealed himself to be the true king by pulling a sword from a stone. The sword was magic, and only the person fit to rule could lift it out. The legend appears in many literary works about King Arthur, such as Sir Thomas Mallory's Le Morte d'Arthur *and T. H. White's* The Once and Future King.

February 13th

I've been practicing all around the castle with my new sword, and I think I'm getting the hang of it now. I've destroyed only four tapestries, three jars, and a chamber pot.

It's a shame the chamber pot was full, as the other stuff was easy to clean up.

Sir Lionel says that although my sword is small, it can still be very deadly, as the sharp end can get through gaps in armor.

I can't wait to get out there and show those Froddington knights what they get for stealing holy fingers.

Except . . .

Seeing as this is a secret diary, I might as well admit something.

I know the Froddington lot shouldn't have stolen the fingers, but it hasn't made me angry enough to kill them.

You can tell from the way Sir Reginald snorts and stamps his feet that he's mad enough to battle our enemies to the death. But I'd be much happier if we could talk them round to returning the fingers without having to actually kill them.

I'm sure this will change when I get out onto the field of battle and see the fiends for myself, though.

February 14th

Tonight's the night I'm getting knighted. Sir Lionel came into my room to talk me through it.

First, I have to bathe in cold water as a symbol

42

that my sins have been washed away. I'm not sure exactly how many sins I've even committed yet. There was that time I stole some honey from the kitchen, I suppose.

Anyway, I'll soon be pure enough to wear a white tunic.

After that comes the tricky bit. I have to go to the chapel, place my sword on the altar, and stay up all night praying.

How am I meant to stay up for the entire night? Will I still be allowed to become a knight if I curl up and drift off for a few hours?

Anyway, after I've stayed up all night, our priest will bless my sword and Sir Lionel will make me a knight.

GET REAL

Dubbing was the final part of the knighthood ceremony. The king, or another knight, would tap the squire on the neck with the flat of a sword. He would then be a knight and could claim the title "sir."

February 15ᵗʰ

I'm so tired right now. I can hardly even see what I'm writing. But I want to get it all down here before I forget the details.

First of all, I am now Sir Roderick. The ceremony went ahead, and I'm officially a knight. Yay!

It didn't exactly go smoothly, though.

First of all, Thomas and Geoffrey were in charge of bathing me, and they made sure the

44

water was really cold. I can take cold baths, but the one they prepared actually had ice on the top. They'd left the tub out overnight to make sure.

I should have ordered them to drag the tub to the fire in the great hall and waited for the ice to melt, but I didn't want to look like a coward, so I jumped in.

Bad idea.

I let out a high scream of fright, which Thomas and Geoffrey thought was the funniest thing they'd ever heard.

As I stood in the freezing tub, rubbing my blue skin and trying to stop my teeth from chattering, Thomas and Geoffrey continued with the next part of their plan to ruin things. They told me the ghost of a headless woman haunts the chapel at night.

Obviously, they were just making up stupid stories because they were jealous. And it completely backfired, because the story frightened me so much I had no problem staying awake all night.

As I knelt before the altar with my sword, I kept imagining a headless lady sneaking up behind me, ready to tap me on the shoulder and

shout "Boo!" Well, probably not that last bit, because you'd need a head for that.

Anyway, I managed to get through the whole night without sleeping, just as I was meant to.

Okay, so technically I was looking around and whimpering rather than praying, but it still counts.

When it was morning, all the others gathered in the chapel and our priest delivered a long sermon about the duties of knighthood. This was the hardest part of all to stay awake through.

When the priest was finally done, he blessed my sword, and Sir Lionel hit me on the shoulder with it. He did it really hard, and I couldn't stop myself from shrieking. But it was too late. I was a knight. They couldn't take the title away now.

After that there was a feast in my honor in the great hall. We had peacock, beef, and swan. It was amazing that such rich foods were brought out in my honor, though some of them smelled a bit off, and I wondered if they were leftovers from Sir Reginald's feast.

But it didn't matter, because Thomas and Geoffrey had to serve me, which automatically made it the best meal ever. The envious losers just had to suck it up. They can make my bath cold and freak me out with stories of headless ghosts, but I'm a knight and they're not, and that's what matters.

After the meal, Leofric came out and told some jokes he'd written especially for the occasion. They were met by silence as usual, but I thought he'd tried pretty hard this time:

"I just got back from Camelot. It was a great place; loved the knight life."

"On my way home, I noticed the peasants were revolting. Don't worry, folks, I'm just talking about the smell."

"It's so great to have Sir Reginald staying with us. But if I were you, Sir Reginald, I'd lay off the feasting for a while. If you don't stop eating soon, you'll have to change your name to Sir Cumfrence."

"But seriously, it's so great to see Roderick becoming a knight today. I find it impossible to praise him too highly. In fact, I find it impossible to praise him at all."

Most people had abandoned the room by the time Leofric was finished, giving me an excuse to slip away for some much-needed sleep.

I think it's time for me to hit the straw. I'm worried that when I wake up I'll find it was all a dream and I'm not really a knight. But I can't keep my eyes open any more.

February 16th

Today I chose my first ever suit of armor. Or at least, I tried to.

Sir Lionel took me to the armory, and I picked out a few pieces. I fixed a greave to my lower leg. It's only meant to cover your shin, but the one I tried came up to my thigh. This would mean I'd have to launch into battle without bending my knees, which wouldn't be great for running.

I tried on a breastplate, which is meant to come down to your waist. It was so low on me it almost touched the greave. There was no room for the cuisses, which are meant to protect the thighs, or the poleyns, which are meant to go over the knees. But there was enough of a gap for an enemy sword to slice me in two. Not much use as armor, then.

Sir Lionel said I was a lot smaller and thinner than most knights. He's going to take a few spare bits of armor to Borin the blacksmith and get him to make a suit that actually fits me.

GET REAL

At first, knights wore small iron rings called mail for armor. But as weapons developed, better protection was needed. Knights began to wear suits of armor made from strong metal plates. They were much heavier than mail, but much more effective.

February 17ᵗʰ

Borin gave me my suit of armor today. At first I was disappointed because the plates he'd made it from didn't match very well. Some of them were new and gleaming, while others were old and rusty, and he'd had to bend them into weird shapes to fit them together. At least the other knights wouldn't need a coat of arms to identify me in battle. They could just look for the knight with the misshapen, mismatched plates.

But I forgot all about how odd the suit looked when I put it on. It fit perfectly, and I found I could move with ease. When I strapped my helmet on and grabbed my sword, I felt ready for any battle.

Get ready to hand the sacred fingers over, Froddington villains. I'm coming for you.

February 18th

I practiced walking around with my suit of armor on today. It's quite heavy, so I thought it would build my muscles if I wore it all the time.

I wandered all around the castle, through the stables, the chapel, the courtyard, and the great hall. I was feeling so confident I decided to go up the spiral staircase on the west of the keep. Getting up wasn't a problem, but coming down was harder. The gap in my visor wasn't big enough for me to see my feet.

I tried to stay near the wall where the stairs are at their widest, but it was still very difficult.

When I was nearly at the bottom, I missed a step. I grasped for the wall but couldn't get a grip on it. I tumbled forward and rolled over five times before clattering to the courtyard floor.

The good news was that my armor gave me excellent protection. Though I'd had the wind knocked out of me, I was sure I hadn't broken any bones. The bad news was that the suit was so heavy I couldn't lift myself up.

It was just as well that all the other knights were in the courtyard and had witnessed my fall. Sir Lionel helped me to my feet, and when the world stopped spinning I saw the others sniggering into their gauntlets.

Sir Reginald was with them. I was really worried that he'd decide Saint Stephen was wrong after all and I shouldn't go on the quest, but he didn't seem to mind.

I told the others I'd deliberately thrown myself down the stairs to test the strength

of my new armor. Then I hobbled back to my
straw and nursed my bruises.

Chapter 4

Tournament Preparations

February 19th

Sir Lionel says I'll be expected to show off my jousting skills at the tournament, and he got really angry when I said I didn't have any. He was the one who was meant to train me in all that stuff. There's no point in getting angry with me for something he should have done.

We took one of the horses out to the field at the front of the castle this afternoon so I could learn.

Sir Lionel helped me get on and handed me a lance.

I never feel very safe on horses. I know that's not a great thing for a new knight to admit. Knights are meant to feel at home on horseback. It should be as comfortable for me as settling down in my straw after a hard day. Instead, I find it scarier than being tapped on the shoulder by a headless ghost.

I'm fine with horses when they're going at a slow canter, but as soon as they speed up I can't stop myself from closing my eyes and sobbing.

I thought things might be different now that I'm a knight, but sadly not.

Sir Lionel set up a long pole with a shield on the end, which he called a quintain. I had to pretend it was my opponent and charge at it.

I held my lance out, put on my fiercest warrior face, and pressed my legs into the sides of the horse.

We set off. The shield was getting closer. We were picking up speed. I felt my fierce warrior

face turn into a fearful wimp one. I dropped the lance and threw my hands over my eyes as the horse raced past the untroubled shield.

We tried again. And again.

Every time the horse got near to a gallop, I closed my eyes, dropped the lance, and wailed.

After I'd done this a few times, I heard laughter coming from the battlements. I looked up and saw that a huge crowd, including Thomas and Geoffrey, had gathered to watch my disastrous training.

Sir Lionel was blushing bright red. He said we should forget the jousting and think of something else I could do to impress the visitors during the tournament, such as play the harp.

February 20th

I went down to the castle dungeons today to chat with Gavin, our prisoner. He's been there since long before I was born, and no one can remember exactly what he did wrong in the first place.

He was on the rack today, laid out on a wooden frame with his ankles and wrists tied to rollers. He asked how I was doing, and I told him I'd been made a knight. He was really pleased, as he knows how much I wanted to be one. I often pop down to see him, and I've mentioned it quite a lot.

I turned the top handle of the rack, wrenching his arms up. He let out a cry of agony and asked me how it was going so far. I told him all about my failed attempts to joust and walk downstairs, and he listened intently between his shrieks of pain.

He said I should just try my best and stop worrying about what other people thought. He explained that when he first became a prisoner, he was terrible at it, begging to be spared from torture and pleading to be set free.

But now he's the best prisoner in the world, and he has a real talent for coping with unbearable pain. He would never have gotten where he is if he'd let other people's opinions get to him.

I think he's right. If I want to be a brilliant knight I can become one, no matter what anyone else says.

I thanked Gavin for his advice as I twisted the bottom handle of the rack, yanking his feet away from his body.

GET REAL

The rack was a grisly medieval torture device. It pulled the victim's arms and legs in opposite directions, sometimes dislocating their joints and tearing their muscles. It was famously used by the Duke of Exeter when he was constable of the Tower of London, and it earned the nickname "The Duke of Exeter's Daughter."

February 21st

I spotted Leofric slumped in the corner of the great hall this morning. I asked him what was wrong, and he said he was jealous of how easily I could make everyone laugh. He said all I have to do is try to walk downstairs or sit on a horse and everyone cracks up. Yet he toils for ages on his gags and no one likes them.

It's weird when you think about it. He wants everyone to laugh at him, but they don't. I don't want everyone to laugh at me, but they do. If only we could swap.

I told him I took great comfort in knowing there's at least one person in the castle worse at their job than me. It didn't seem to cheer him up.

Leofric's next performance will be at the feast following the tournament, and he's worried about going down like a cup of cold dragon sick again.

I helped him come up with some new jokes, and I think they're better than his previous ones. The new material is all about the Froddington knights. Everyone really hates them, so it will be much easier to get the crowd going with stuff about them.

Here are the new gags we came up with:

"What do you call ten dead Froddington knights? A good start."

"Why did God invent Froddington knights? So peasants would have someone to look down on."

"What's the difference between a Froddington knight and a full chamber pot? The chamber pot."

I told him to keep working on the Froddington material and he was bound to get laughs.

February 22nd

Disaster averted. We've sorted out the whole tournament thing. In addition to the jousting, there's going to be a javelin contest. It's really simple. You have to throw a spear as far as you can. It's a really useful skill in battle, as you can pick off enemies from a safe distance.

All I have to do is throw the javelin farther than all the others from our castle, and it won't look weird that they made me a knight.

Sir Lionel took me out to the fields behind the castle to see how far I could throw. He said he'd fix the contest to make sure I beat everyone else.

I threw the javelin over and over again, and it kept hitting the same spot just a few feet ahead. Sir Lionel seemed really surprised I couldn't get it farther and said it would be really difficult for the other knights to avoid beating me.

They'll just have to think of a convincing way to mess up their attempts. Maybe they can all sneeze or fall over as they throw or something.

It doesn't matter. The main thing is I'm going to win a contest and look brilliant in front of a massive crowd. Can't wait.

Chapter 5
Girl Trouble

February 23rd

The Bamwell knights arrived this morning and some had members of their families with them. My eye was immediately caught by Isolde, the daughter of a knight called Sir Maurice.

She's my age, a little taller than me, and has blue eyes and long blonde hair. She was wearing a green dress and one of those trendy steeple hats.

I might as well admit it here in my secret diary–I fancy her. And now that I'm a dashing knight, she's bound to fancy me too.

But when Sir Reginald introduced me to her this morning, I found I'd somehow forgotten how to speak, and all that came out of my mouth were weird stuttering sounds.

I thought capturing a maiden's heart would be

easy now that I'm a knight. Apparently not. I'd better ask Sir Lionel for advice.

February 24ᵗʰ

Sir Lionel said the best way to impress a lady is to go on quests in her name. He says a knight should go anywhere and do anything to prove his love and dedicate all his brave deeds to the lady.

Sounds simple enough. I just need to carry out some courageous errands in Isolde's name and her heart will be mine.

February 25ᵗʰ

I spotted Isolde in the courtyard this afternoon and asked if I could do anything for her. She said I could fetch her steeple hat, which she'd accidentally left in her room.

I declared I was fetching it in her name, and I thought this would be enough to make her swoon, but she didn't react. I heroically strode up to the guest rooms, found her bonnet, and brought it back. I didn't even fall downstairs this time.

I asked her if there was anything else I could do to prove myself, and she said I could get Thomas to come and speak to her because she thought he was really good-looking.

Sigh!

73

I'm not going on that quest in her name.

She totally failed to understand my feelings, and now I'm wondering if Sir Lionel's advice was worth following at all.

Never mind. The tournament is tomorrow. All I need to do is win my event and dedicate my victory to her. Then my feelings will be clear and she will be mine.

GET REAL

The romantic idea of courtly love was important to knights in the Middle Ages. They would go to great lengths to prove their love for noble women, from going without food and sleep to battling rivals.

February 26th

Let's just say today didn't go brilliantly.

We had a wonderful, bright day for the tournament, and I felt confident as I strode over to the wooden stands we'd put up at the front of the castle. I sat behind Isolde and her father and watched our lot take on Bamwell in the jousting. Some idiots were complaining about me not taking part, even though the whole tournament was being held in my honor. I didn't worry about it, because I knew my astounding performance in the javelin would silence them.

Although the jousters used lances with blunt ends, so none of them were actually killed, a few of them had very painful falls, and I was glad I'd got out of it.

Isolde muttered something to her dad about how brave the knights were, and I felt a bit jealous. But I was too giddy with excitement about my upcoming moment of glory to care much.

Soon it was time for my big moment. I stepped down from the stands and stood with our knights on the field.

Sir Lionel had lodged a pebble on the ground to show the others how far I could throw, so they knew not to beat it.

One by one our knights went through their pathetic throws. It looked like it was quite hard for them to do so badly. Over on the stands, some of the Bamwell knights were looking confused.

I gazed at Isolde as she winced at the poor attempts of the other knights. Soon I would storm the contest, and she'd see me for the hero I was.

Sir Hugh took his turn, aiming the javelin straight down and getting it just a couple of feet forward. There were boos from the crowd.

Now it was my turn.

Sir Lionel fetched the javelin from the ground and handed it to me. I held it over my shoulder, took a deep breath, and took a run up to the starting line. The pebble was right ahead. I just had to get the javelin over that and I'd win. Just as I was about to release the javelin, I remembered I'd meant to dedicate my victory to Isolde. I turned to the left so I could see the

stands. I picked out her beautiful face and shouted, "This is for you!"

Then something terrible happened. My arm accidentally threw the javelin while I was still facing the stand. Instead of flying toward the pebble, it sped over to my beloved Isolde.

It was just my luck. Every time I'd tried to throw the spear as far as I could, it had flopped straight down. Now I didn't want it to go far and it was soaring over to the stands.

Isolde leapt aside and screamed as the javelin struck the place where she'd been sitting.

Sir Lionel managed to cover it well. He said I'd proved my strength by throwing the javelin all the way to the stands, and with power like that, we'd have no trouble teaching the Froddington swine a lesson.

79

The other knights gave a rousing round cheer, and the Bamwell knights did their best to join in.

Isolde didn't look impressed. She glared at me as she straightened her steeple hat and smoothed down her dress.

The uncomfortable atmosphere continued during the banquet, and I spotted several of the Bamwell lot pointing at me and muttering.

Things felt really awkward by the time Leofric did his jokes about the Froddington knights, and his act went down just as badly as usual. It was a real shame because I thought he did quite well. It just wasn't a great time to perform. Even the best jesters in the country couldn't have gotten a laugh today.

February 27th

I was worried Sir Reginald might have changed his mind about taking me on the quest after yesterday's disaster, but this morning he told me to get ready to depart.

He made no mention of my little mishap and doesn't seem to regret making me a knight. Sir Reginald is a man of great faith and if Saint Stephen tells him to do something, he does it.

It's just as well. If he listened to reason rather than old, dead saints, he'd put me straight back on plate-washing duties. I've got a lot to thank Sir Reginald and Saint Stephen for. And I fully intend to repay their confidence by grabbing the holy shriveled digits.

I could sit around moping about how I messed up my training and how I almost speared the girl I love with a javelin. But I'm not going to. I'm going to get out there and be a fantastic knight.

Bring it on.

February 28ᵗʰ

Today Sir Reginald told me there was still one important thing I had to do before we set off on the quest. I got worried that I'd have to pull a sword out of a stone or something tricky, but I just had to listen to him talking about chivalry.

It was much easier than staying awake all night or charging at a foe on horseback.

We stood on top of the east tower, looking out at the forest while Sir Reginald chewed on a leg of pork and delivered his lecture.

He said knights should always be brave, but they should act with honor too. Any smelly old warrior can fight an enemy, but a true knight respects him too. A knight must never attack an enemy from behind, and he must always spare his life if he surrenders. A knight must also be loyal to his friends, keep his promises, and be polite.

I asked him if he thought the Froddington knights were chivalrous, and he said he hoped so. When we arrive at their castle, we'll march up to their gatehouse and ask for the fingers back before trying anything like scaling the wall and overpowering everyone.

I hope the quest ends up being as easy as that. We turn up to their door, we ask for the fingers back, they hand them over to us, and we return as heroes. Something tells me that's not going to happen, though.

Chapter 6

—

We Set Off on a Quest

March I*st*

Our quest has begun.

We set off at dawn and everyone from the castle
turned out to see us. I waved at Leofric and told
him to keep working on new material. I tried
to wave at Isolde, but she scowled and turned
away. I was even chivalrous enough to wave
at Thomas and Geoffrey, though all they could
manage to do in return was cheer in a sarcastic
way. I told them they'd have to learn to be more
chivalrous if they wanted to become knights.

Soon we were away, trotting through the forest
to the east of the castle. I rode at the front with
Sir Lionel and got him to tell me some Knights
of the Round Table stories. He knows loads, and
they're great for passing the time.

He told me how King Arthur was given his
sword by a lady in a lake, even though I'm

pretty sure he was meant to have pulled it out of a stone instead. This is why I'm writing all my heroic deeds down. When people tell stories about me in the future, they won't have to argue about details like where I got my sword.

He told me about how Sir Lancelot crawled across a bridge made from a blade to rescue Queen Guinevere. I'd like to think I'd do the same for Isolde if the situation ever arises. I hope it doesn't though. It sounds like it would really sting.

And he told me about the seat at the round table that the magician Merlin reserved for the greatest knight of all. If an unworthy knight sat on it, he'd be burned to death by a pillar of fire. Sir Lancelot sat on it and he was fine, showing that he was the best. It sounds like an even more frightening way of proving yourself than jousting.

88

I hope people do tell stories about me one day.
Obviously, I don't want to go quite as far as the
Knights of the Round Table. But I'd be prepared
to sit in an especially hot bath, or crawl across
a really blunt blade.

March 2nd

We rode over flat plains today, which meant
our horses could go much faster. This made me
yelp with fright, and mine panicked and bolted
away. Sir Lionel had to ride over and guide it
back to the others.

After this had happened a few times, Sir Hugh
got really angry and said I was already ruining
their quest with my cowardice and we weren't
anywhere near the enemy.

I told him it wasn't very chivalrous to be rude
to a fellow knight, and he went purple and said

he wasn't going to be lectured in chivalry by a pipsqueak who couldn't even complete a quest to the bottom of a stairwell.

I bet Arthur had to put up with that sort of nonsense until he yanked his sword out of a stone or grabbed it from the lady in the lake or whatever he actually did. I hope I get a moment like that soon so they all stop criticizing me.

When we set off again I totally managed to stop screaming, and my horse found it much easier. But did any of the other knights congratulate me?

No. None of them even mentioned it. Typical.

March 3rd

Every time we pass a group of peasants, Sir Hugh shouts rude things at them. He teases them for being poor and smelly and tells them to go back to their ditches and stop spreading the plague.

Sir Lionel always tells him to stop provoking the peasants in case they rise up against the rest of us and steal all our stuff.

Sir Hugh finds this hilarious and says peasants are stupid animals and are no more likely than dogs to rise up against us.

It's an interesting discussion, and I think I'm on Sir Lionel's side. There are more of them than there are of us, and if they ever worked that out they could overthrow everyone. It would only take one peasant who was good at public speaking to convince the others to revolt.

On the other hand, they're so tired from working all day and not eating much, they're unlikely to try anything soon.

Teasing them about their unfortunate position isn't going to help matters, though.

GET REAL

There were several uprisings of downtrodden peasants in the Middle Ages. The most famous, which is often called "The Peasants' Revolt," was led by Wat Tyler in 1381. They objected to the poll tax, which had been brought in to fund the war with France, and they didn't want to work for free on church land. The revolt ended when Tyler was stabbed by the Lord Mayor of London, William Walworth.

March 4th

We passed a troubadour today. He had on a
red jacket and black hat and was carrying a
lute. He was on his way to perform at a feast
but stopped and sang for us when Sir Reginald
offered him a coin.

We got off our horses and settled on the ground
while the troubadour did "The Song of Roland."

The sun broke through the clouds as he
performed, and for the first time since we'd set

off I was truly glad I'd come along. But then the story got quite scary, and I started to worry about our quest again.

There's a bit in the song where Roland and his troops are going into battle and he refuses to blow on his horn to get help from the rest of the army. He gets killed, and we're all meant to think he's really brave for choosing to fight when the odds are stacked against him. I just thought he was silly.

There were some really gory descriptions of battles, and it made me hope we don't push ahead and fight if we're seriously outnumbered by the Froddington knights.

No one makes up songs about you if you start crying and run away. But you do get to still be alive, and that's kind of a better option.

March 5ᵗʰ

We stopped for lunch in a field today, and a group of peasants carrying huge piles of wood hobbled past. They all had grubby black teeth, muddy hair, and sores on their faces.

Sir Hugh threatened to chop their heads off if they didn't leave us alone, so they waddled off. I felt sorry for them so I walked after them and tried to make conversation.

I asked them what the wood was for, and they said it was for their lord's fire. I asked what their lord was like and they said he was quite fair. He let them use the manure from his animals to coat their houses, and he even let them have the straw from his stables if it was already infected with lice.

I patted one of the men on the shoulder and said I was sorry to hear about their mean lord and I wished them luck in their struggle.

For some reason they seemed to find this hilarious and kept repeating it to each other in what I think was meant to be my accent.

I can't believe I got mocked for trying to reach out to those less fortunate than myself. Just my luck.

GET REAL

Medieval society was divided into a feudal system. The king was at the top, followed by wealthy nobles such as lords. Knights were beneath them, but they could become rich enough to buy their own land. At the bottom of the system were the hardworking peasants who lived a tough and often miserable existence.

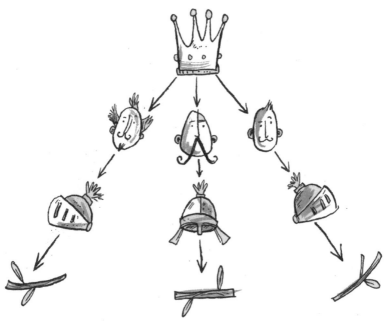

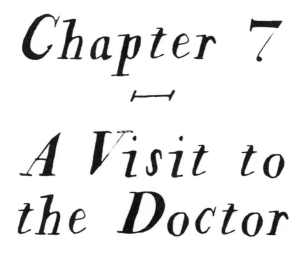

Chapter 7

A Visit to the Doctor

March 6ᵗʰ

Everyone has been teasing me for trying to
make friends with the peasants yesterday. Sir
Hugh said they probably had the plague, and
I'll have caught it when I tapped one of them on
the back.

I pretended I wasn't bothered by his silly lies,
but he went on and on about what the plague
was going to do to me.

He said black blotches would erupt on my skin
and I'd get swellings over my body that would
leak blood and pus. I'd feel cold, then hot, then
I'd get a headache, and then I'd drop down
dead.

Since he said that this morning I've felt cold,
then hot, and gotten a headache. Of course, this
might have been because it rained, then the sun
came out, and then I got sick from worrying I
might have the plague.

But I'm not going to let Sir Hugh get to me. I haven't got any black marks on my skin, and I'm not oozing pus, so I know I'm fine, really.

Oh God. What if I've got the plague?

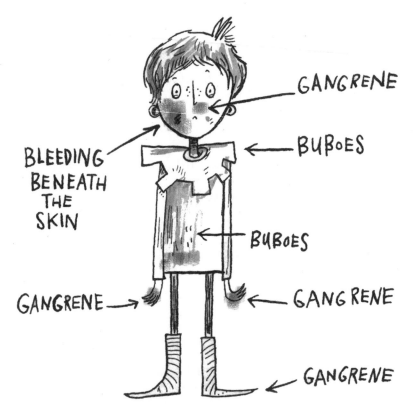

GET REAL

The outbreak of bubonic plague in the late Middle Ages has become known as the "Black Death." It swept through Europe in the middle of the 14th century, killing a third of the population. Many people believed they were being punished by God for their sins. We now know the plague was spread by fleas carried by rats.

March 7th

We stopped at a village called Foddleshire today. The knights went to the local tavern, while I went to search for a doctor. Sir Hugh's teasing about my plague symptoms was getting to me and I wanted a checkup.

The locals told me to visit a man called Tristan, who was the village doctor and barber. I had to sit outside his shop waiting for a man to get his curly hair trimmed before he could see me.

I told Tristan about how I'd felt cold, then hot, and then gotten a headache, and he examined me. He told me I didn't have the plague, but my body's fluids were out of balance and he could restore them for a bargain price.

I figured I might as well get it done, so I handed over a coin. Tristan grabbed my arm, took out a tiny blade, and sliced open one of my veins. He held my bleeding arm over a bowl and asked if we were going anywhere nice on our trip. I didn't feel like chatting as I was already quite busy weeping with pain.

At least none of the other knights saw that.

When the bowl was full, he gave me my arm back and asked if I needed anything else. Apparently he gave great discounts on hair trims and amputations to all his bloodletting customers.

I decided to leap out of the shop while I still had legs.

I was feeling really weak by the time I got back to the others, and I kept stumbling. I thought they might have been sympathetic, but they seemed to think it was hilarious. Sir Robert said I must have been drinking the same stuff as they were, which was apparently the funniest thing anyone had ever said.

GET REAL

Bloodletting was a popular treatment for many illnesses in the Middle Ages. It was based on the ancient Greek idea that good health needs a balance of blood, phlegm, yellow bile, and black bile. If someone was ill, it meant he or she had too much blood and some should be removed. The practice survived for centuries, even though it was often very harmful to patients.

March 8th

We had a full day of riding, and I still felt terrible after my trip to the so-called doctor. I kept flopping to the side and almost falling off.

At one point I blacked out and had this really vivid dream that I had the plague and I needed to hit Saint Stephen's fingers with a javelin to cure myself. I screamed myself awake, which sent my horse bolting away from the rest again.

All day I've been switching back and forth between fever and panic. I thought quests would be a nonstop procession of chivalry and fun. I just wish I was back at the castle tucked up in my comfy straw.

March 9th

I felt even worse today. If Sir Hugh hadn't scared me about catching the plague, I'd never have seen that useless doctor.

I don't know what I was thinking. Going to the doctor never works.

Whenever I used to go to the castle doctor, Cedric, complaining of a headache or a stomachache, he'd poke me with a red-hot iron, stick leeches on me, and make me drink disgusting potions made from herbs and weird bits of animals.

After a while I realized staying in my straw was a better option. At least that way I wouldn't end up with a leech on my chest and the taste of dried hedgehog in my mouth.

GET REAL

Doctors in the Middle Ages used all sorts of treatments that seem crazy now. Medical knowledge was generally based on superstition rather than scientific proof. Illnesses were sometimes blamed on things such as the movement of the stars and demons trapped inside the body. Some doctors believed the best way to cure an ailing part of the body was to eat something that resembled it. For example, walnuts were said to cure headaches because they looked like heads.

March 10th

I finally felt better again today. The sun came out, and we spent most of the day racing over flat ground. I'm much more used to high speeds now, and I hardly screamed at all.

I was almost beginning to relax and enjoy myself. But then Sir Reginald announced we'd be arriving at Froddington Castle tomorrow, and everyone went on about how they couldn't wait to fight the other knights.

The conversation soon turned into a boasting contest about brave deeds. Sir Hugh told us about the time he killed twelve foot soldiers with his lance.

Sir Robert described the time he was cut off from his army and surrounded by enemy soldiers carrying sharp sticks so he couldn't

charge at them. He dismounted and killed
every single one of them with just his dagger.

Sir Lionel told us how he'd scaled the wall of a
castle using a ladder and killed thirty guards.

But they all fell silent when Sir Reginald
spoke. He's the only one of the knights who's
actually been over to the Holy Land to fight.
That's much more impressive than attacking
a rival bunch of knights.

He's even met the Knights Templar, the
toughest warriors in the whole world. He
says they hunt lions instead of boars and go
for ages without food to prove how much they
love God. But even when they're in a starved
and weakened state, they can still beat
anyone in a fight.

At least we've only got to battle those Froddington cowards and not tough guys like the Knights Templar.

No one spoke for ages after Sir Reginald had finished, and I considered telling them all about the time I beat Geoffrey at chess three times in one day. But something told me I couldn't quite compete.

GET REAL

Between 1095 and 1291, many knights traveled to the Holy Land, modern-day Israel and Palestine, to fight in the Crusades. These were holy wars waged between Christians and Muslims. The Knights Templar were formed to help Christian pilgrims get to Jerusalem. They followed strict rules and gave themselves harsh punishments if they broke them.

Chapter 8

⊢——⊣

Things Don't Go According to Plan

March 11^(th)

We're sitting on a hill overlooking Froddington
Castle now. The sun is setting, and we're going
to wait until tomorrow morning to take back
Saint Stephen's fingers.

Froddington Castle isn't quite as big as ours,
but it looks pretty secure. It has a keep inside
a large courtyard surrounded by a curtain wall
with six flanking towers. There are overhanging
bits on the towers with holes in the bottom,
so they can drop stuff on anyone who tries to
attack. There's a gatehouse at the entrance,
with a heavy portcullis gate, and the whole
castle is surrounded by a deep ditch.

I asked Sir Reginald what his military strategy
for taking the castle was if the knights don't
give in to our demands. He said we don't need
one because we've got Saint Stephen on our
side and he'll look out for us. He didn't say how

he expects him to do it, but it probably involves him appearing in a cloud and threatening the Froddington lot with bolts of lightning if they don't give in.

Oh God, we're all going to die tomorrow, aren't we?

Never mind. At least I'll get to find out what it's like to be a bold knight, even if it's only for the few seconds from when we ask for the fingers back to when the Froddington knights attack.

March 12th

We're still alive, which is a nice surprise.

What's less surprising is that the Froddington knights weren't too keen on giving us Saint Stephen's fingers, and the old saint himself didn't show up.

We approached the castle just after dawn, and by the time we were at the gatehouse, several knights were looking down at us from the battlements.

Sir Reginald rode up to the closed portcullis and announced that we were the knights of Doddingford Castle, here to claim the fingers of Saint Stephen so we could return them to Yellowfriars Monastery.

The Froddington knights told us to retreat or die. Then there were a few awkward minutes of silence where Sir Reginald stared up at the clouds. I think this was Saint Stephen's cue to show up.

Unfortunately, this just gave the Froddington villains a chance to prepare their attack. Boiling water came gushing out of one of the castle's holes onto Sir Reginald's helmet.

He yelped with pain and took it off, revealing his red, scowling face. Now the knights fired arrows down at Sir Reginald, aiming for his exposed head.

Sir Reginald ordered us to retreat, and the fiends kept up their onslaught as we raced away. I felt arrows thudding off my back and was grateful the blacksmith had done such a good job on my suit. If he'd left any gaps between the plates, I'd have a few nasty holes in my back right now.

So much for knights always being polite and never attacking an enemy from behind. I guess this means the Froddington knights aren't the chivalrous kind.

We're back on the hill now. Unless Saint Stephen destroys the gatehouse with a freak flash of lightning, we're going to need a plan.

GET REAL

Some castles had walls that jutted out at the top, leaving a gap called a machicolation. These were used to drop things such as stones and boiling water on attackers. Similar holes in the ceilings of gateways and passageways were called murder holes.

March 13th

Our band of knights may be fearless in battles, but they're also clueless in planning them.

All day they've been discussing how to get Saint Stephen's fingers back, and we're no closer to agreeing on anything.

Sir Robert thinks we should tunnel our way into the Froddington courtyard and storm

the chapel. This is a terrible idea, as the
castle sits in the middle of a wide, flat plain.
They can see for miles around from their
towers. We'd have to go down to the other
side of the hill we're currently on and tunnel
for over a mile to get into the courtyard. We'd
all be as old and decrepit as Saint Stephen's
fingers themselves by the time we got there.

Sir Lionel thinks we should search for a large
tree that could make a battering ram. I didn't
want to be disloyal to him, so I didn't say
anything, but I thought this was also a bad
idea. The portcullis would be far too strong
to break. There are a couple of sections of the
wall that might be quite weak, but they're
surrounded by the ditch, so we wouldn't be
able to get a good run at them. No doubt we'd
just make a spectacle of ourselves at the base
of the castle while boiling water and arrows
showered down.

Sir Hugh had the worst plan of all. He suggested we chop down some trees, build a catapult, and fire ME into the courtyard. Once inside, I'd get up, dust myself off, and launch an attack on the Froddington knights. I'm sure I'd die from breaking all my bones before I even had a chance to get killed by the enemy.

Sir Hugh said he'd love to do it himself, but I'd be able to fly farther, as I was smaller and lighter. Yeah, right.

Even if someone had come up with a decent plan, Sir Reginald would have ignored them. He's convinced Saint Stephen himself is going to pop down and bail us out. Every time there's a break in the clouds, he wipes a tear from his eye and shouts, "You've arrived!"

The rest of us look around in awkward silence as Sir Reginald realizes there are no giant saints in the sky.

March 14th

If you can't overpower your rivals, you need to outwit them. In our case, we're trying to get inside a castle with good defenses. No matter how brave and strong we are, the Froddington knights will have the advantage.

So we'll have to trick them into handing the fingers over. Maybe we could dig up some dead bodies from a plague pit and make some fake relics to trade. I'm sure they'd swap at least a couple of the fingers if we said we had the knee of Saint Peter or the armpit of John the Baptist.

This method might have worked if we'd started with it. But now that we've admitted we want the fingers, they'll know exactly what's going on if we suddenly remember we've brought a bag of top-quality relics with us.

Maybe if we can get inside the castle under other pretenses we can swipe the fingers from their chapel while they're asleep. We could claim to be a traveling band of troubadours and offer to entertain them in exchange for a place to stay.

124

No, that's not going to work. Even if the others took off their armor, it would be obvious from their battle scars and scowling faces that they're knights.

None of us could pass for anyone other than a knight. Except for me.

Wait! I've got it! I could go on my own. Nobody thinks I look like a knight. If I take my armor off and rub mud on myself, no one will ever suspect I am one. I could offer my services as an ordinary worker in exchange for somewhere to sleep, and then snatch the fingers when no one is around . . .

March 15^{*th*}

The others were still arguing when I tried to tell them my brilliant plan, and I couldn't get a word in.

But it's not as if I need them anyway. I could sneak off and fetch the fingers while they're still bickering.

If they still haven't made their minds up by tonight, I'm going down to the castle whether they listen to me or not.

Chapter 9

My Daring
Solo Mission

March 16ᵗʰ

The others were no nearer to an agreement last night, so I went ahead on my own.

I wandered down to the bottom of the hill and found a patch of long grass. I took my armor off and rubbed mud all over myself.

I was glad I'd made the effort to speak to those peasants the other day, because it meant I could copy their accents, hunched posture, and expression of despair.

I hobbled up to the gatehouse and called for the guard. I told him I was a poor peasant looking for work in exchange for food and shelter. He told me to go away and take my plague with me.

I promised I was free of all diseases and lice and stressed I'd do any job at all if they'd give me a stale crust of bread and somewhere to sleep. He said he'd ask around, but he couldn't promise anything.

He returned a couple of minutes later and checked that I really was prepared to do any job at all. I nodded, and he said they needed a new night soil man. I said I had loads of experience with night soil and I'd love to do it. The man shrugged and left his post. A few moments later, the portcullis rose, and he showed me in.

I stepped across the courtyard toward the keep. I spotted a small chapel to my right. No doubt that's where the fingers were. But the courtyard was packed with blacksmiths, grooms, and candlemakers. I'd have to wait until later to steal them.

The guard warned me they hadn't been able to find a night soil man for a few weeks, so I'd have to work through until morning to clear the backlog. But he promised me an especially big chunk of stale bread if I could still keep food down when I was finished.

I couldn't believe my luck. They'd given me a job I could quietly get on with until everyone was asleep. Then I could grab the fingers and escape with no one watching.

The guard led me to a narrow stairway that went under the east side of the keep. He pointed to a wooden cart and told me to fill it by morning. He said I could empty it into the moat if I liked, as long as I kept it away from the gatehouse where he had to stand. Then he pointed down the stairs and said I should be able to find a shovel in there somewhere.

A tangy smell wafted up and made my eyes water. As I plodded down the steps, the horrible truth dawned on me. "Night soil" was their term for poo. I was stepping into the cesspit where all the waste from the castle toilet fell.

Oh well. I could hardly turn back now.

I took a deep breath and waded into the brown sludge.

Flies swarmed up to my face. My feet didn't touch ground until the vile waste was over my knees. I stuck a hand into the pungent dirt and felt around until I struck the handle of a shovel.

I pulled it out and held it aloft like a stinky King Arthur. It was time to begin.

I loaded the shovel with poo and lugged it up the stairs. I sploshed it into the wooden cart and went back down for another helping of poo. The guard hadn't been joking when he'd said it would take until morning to fill the cart.

But if I could do it before then, I'd have an excuse to take it outside the castle while there was still no one around, and make my escape. I'd have to push myself to my limits to get it done on time.

I hurried up and down the stairs over and over
again until a small brown pool covered the
bottom of the cart. The sun set and the moon
rose high in the sky, and still I continued my
disgusting task.

The castle eventually fell silent except for
distant snoring and chatter. I kept on trekking
up and down the stairs.

I forced myself to keep going, my heart lifting
every time I emptied the shovel.

Finally, when it was almost dawn, the poo level
was at the top of the cart.

I checked that no one was around and rushed
into the chapel. There was a wooden box on
the altar with three cloth bags inside. The first
contained ears, the second contained teeth, but

the third contained bony grey fingers. I grabbed it and stuffed in under my tunic.

I went back to my cart and wheeled it over to the front gate. Poo slopped over the sides and sploshed onto the courtyard as I went.

There was a different guard on duty above
the gatehouse now. He stared at me with his
small dark eyes as I approached.

I remembered to put on my peasant voice and
told him I had to empty my cart as it was full,
and I'd never get through the backlog of night
soil if I stopped until morning.

He said he was under strict orders to keep the
gate closed ever since a weird group of rival
knights had turned up to try to steal some
important relic or other.

I told him I knew nothing about knights or
any of that fancy stuff, but I knew my cart
was full, and I had strict orders of my own
to obey.

He shrugged and said there was nothing
he could do.

I stroked my chin for a second and then told him
I'd had an idea. He could help me carry my cart
up to the top of the gatehouse and we could tip
it into the moat together. Of course, some of the
night soil would spill on his clothes, and onto the
area where he worked, and it would all smear
down the front of the castle, but it would be
better than going against his orders.

He glanced from side to side, then left his post to
raise the portcullis. He hissed at me to be quick
and keep what he'd done a secret.

When I was out I trundled round to the west of
the castle. When I was sure I was out of sight,
I ditched the cart and dashed back to the grass
where I'd hidden my armor.

I'm back with the others now, but they're all
asleep. I think I'll get a couple of hours' rest too
before telling them the good news.

March 17th

I woke up this morning to find the others standing over me. Sir Robert said I smelled like I'd had an accident, and Sir Hugh said the excitement of the trip must have been too much for me.

I leapt to my feet and pulled the fingers out from under my tunic. The others looked confused. I suppose it can't have been entirely obvious why I was covered in poo and holding up a bag.

When I told them they were looking at Saint Stephen's fingers, Sir Reginald threw himself to the ground and declared it a miracle. He said the saint had come down from heaven in the night, hidden the fingers under my tunic, and smeared poo all over me.

I told them all how I'd tricked the guard into letting me in and how I'd got the fingers. The others were all very impressed, except for Sir Hugh and Sir Robert, who were annoyed they wouldn't get a chance to try out their ridiculous plans.

Instead of thanking me for saving the day, Sir Reginald thanked Saint Stephen for putting the wonderful plan in my head. I can't believe Saint Stephen even gets the credit this time.

I handed the fingers over to Sir Reginald and he examined them and confirmed they were genuine. While the others were fawning over them, I glanced down at the castle and noticed some of the guards were examining the poo cart I'd abandoned. It wouldn't be long before they worked out the fingers were missing and came out to attack.

As soon as they did, I'd have no chance of getting everyone to flee. They'd stay and fight to the death, even if we were massively outnumbered.

I told the others we had to return to our castle right away and share the news of our triumph.

March 18th

We covered loads of ground today, racing over the fields from before dawn until after dusk.

I'm finding some of the riding quite frightening, especially when my horse leaps over ditches and I have to cling on really tight. But I'm trying my best not to wail with fright and make my horse run away from the pack.

For all I know, the Froddington knights could be on our trail right now. And battling them would be much scarier than riding fast.

I just need to shut my eyes and cling on and it will all be over soon.

March 22nd

We're back in the castle now. Everyone rushed out to greet us, and when Sir Lionel told them I'd rescued the fingers they all cheered.

Some of the squires came over to hug me, but they ran away again as soon as they smelled me. It's not my fault we didn't have time to stop for a bath.

Anyway, I've washed now and put a new tunic on.

Everywhere I go, people stop and get me to tell them the story of how I stole the fingers. I make sure I tell it especially loudly if Thomas and Geoffrey are around. They've been trying to ignore me, but I can tell they're really jealous of all the attention I'm getting.

Brother Fendrel, one of the monks from Yellowfriars, is on his way round to pick up the fingers. In the meantime, the knights of Bamwell are coming back and we're having a feast to celebrate our victory. I really hope

Isolde comes. She's bound to be impressed when she finds out what I did.

But right now the exhaustion is catching up with me. It will be so nice to get back to my comfy straw after all that time roughing it outdoors.

March 23rd

I went down to the dungeons to see our prisoner Gavin this afternoon. He was really pleased to hear about my role in our victory.

I asked him how things had been going for him, and he said he'd spent some time in the Judas Chair, some time on the rack, and some time in the boot. It's good that they've been giving him a variety of tortures. I know how he prides himself on being able to withstand all the different types.

He was on the thumbscrews today, so I tightened them as I told him all about my experiences with the troubadour, the peasants, and the doctor along the way to Froddington.

GET REAL

Many horrific torture devices were used in medieval dungeons, often to try to make prisoners confess their crimes. The Judas Chair had tight straps and was layered with hundreds of sharp metal spikes. The boot was made from narrow boards of wood fixed around the victim's leg. Additional wedges of wood were hammered into it, crushing their feet. Thumbscrews were small metal vices that crushed the victim's fingernails.

*March 24*th

The Bamwell knights arrived this evening, and the great news is that Isolde was with them. She was wearing a green dress and a steeple hat that was even taller than her last one. She has to bend down to get through doorways now.

She came over and congratulated me for being brave on the adventure. It would have been the perfect time for me to say something romantic, but my mind went blank and I blushed bright red. You'd think it would be much easier for me to talk to girls now that I'm a hero, but apparently it's as tough as ever.

I found Sir Lionel afterward and asked him for advice. He said that even the bravest knights find it frightening to express their feelings.

But then he told me about a brilliant way round it. All you have to do is write love poetry. That way you can get your noble emotions down first and you only have to worry about reading them out loud when your fair lady is around.

He said the best way to write love poetry is to compare your love to a serious battle injury. That way you can show her how brave and how romantic you are at the same time.

Sounds straightforward enough. I'll get working on it.

March 25*th*

I really enjoyed the feast today. Everyone was talking about my brilliant plan, and loads of the Bamwell knights apologized to Sir Reginald for doubting his decision to knight me.

He said it just went to show that you should always follow instructions given in visions. Saint Stephen wanted his fingers to go back to Yellowfriars, and he knew I could play a vital role in stealing them.

While we were eating, Leofric came out and did some topical material he'd written about our quest:

"It's so great to hear you've brought Saint Stephen's fingers back. I think you all deserve a hand. And you've already got part of one."

"We're all relieved Saint Stephen's fingers are back. Especially Saint Stephen himself, who has an itchy nose."

"But seriously, it's great to have them back. I haven't been so worried about missing ancient relics since I lost my joke book."

Leofric's gags still didn't go down very well, but I laughed really loudly to make him feel better. Most of the others started chatting after the first couple of jokes, except for Sir Reginald, who scowled and went red. I think he was angry that Leofric was joking about something he takes so seriously.

All throughout the feast I kept glancing at Isolde, who was at the far end of the table to my left. It took me ages to pluck up the courage to read my poem to her. I waited until everyone was talking really loudly so they wouldn't hear me, and then I stepped over.

I clutched my scrap of paper in my trembling hands and read my poem:

Like a dagger in my ankle
Like a mace up my nose
Like a spear in my eyeball
Like an axe through my toes
Your love has left me wounded
And whimpering with pain
But my suffering is brilliant
Please beat me up again.

As soon as I started, all the other conversations stopped. Everyone turned to listen as I read out my heartfelt words. I think my poem must have affected a lot of the others, because I could see them blushing and wincing. Some of them even looked as though they were holding back tears, or maybe laughter.

Isolde didn't know what to say when I'd

finished, and I'm not surprised with everyone staring like that.

I went back to my seat and the conversation gradually picked up again. I'm pretty sure I won her heart. I just wish I'd read my poem somewhere private enough for her to have told me afterward.

*March 26*th

Brother Fendrel came round for the fingers this afternoon. Tomorrow he's going back to Yellowfriars with Sir Reginald. It makes me so proud to think that, thanks to me, the fingers will soon be back in the monastery's relic collection next to John the Baptist's liver and Saint Paul's earlobe.

It was a tough quest, but it all turned out fine in the end.

Chapter 10
—
Under Attack!

March 27ᵗʰ

This is a disaster! The knights from
Froddington are attacking us!

They sneaked up on our guards this morning,
scaling the east and west towers with massive
ladders. They were hoping to storm the castle,
kill us all in our sleep, and make off with
the fingers.

Luckily our guards were too good for them. They pushed both ladders down to the ground before any of the Froddington knights had reached the top, leaving the fiends winded and flailing on the ground.

Soon we were all lining the wall, gatehouse, and towers, firing arrows and chucking boiling water at the enemy. They retreated, no doubt to plan their next cowardly attack.

I counted twenty-three Froddington knights. They must really want the fingers back. It's just as well the Bamwell knights are here to help us defend against the villains.

March 28th

I barely slept all night. Every time I settled down on my straw, I imagined the Froddington knights scaling the walls and rampaging through the castle. I'd have to leap to my feet and defend everyone if that happened. I don't think I'd get away with hiding down in the dungeons with Gavin now that I'm a knight.

By dawn it became clear the Froddington lot weren't going to try anything just yet.

There was a meeting for all us knights this morning and Sir Lionel suggested we ride out and pursue the Froddington knights.

I was waiting for someone to say this was a bad idea and we should stay here and see what happens. No one did.

Sir Reginald nodded. He said there were twenty-four of us, including the Bamwell knights, so we outnumbered them by one and hunting them down would be the right thing to do.

I can't believe I'm the extra knight making a difference in our numbers. I'm surprised I even count toward the total.

We're setting out tomorrow to hunt down the enemy. Sir Reginald gave us a lecture about all the sneaky tactics they could use when we meet them in battle.

He said that dishonest foes like the Froddington lot sometimes draw you into a battlefield filled with hidden holes. Your horse trips as it charges through, so you crash to the ground and they surround you. Or they might get you to follow them into a dense forest where archers are waiting in the trees.

The Froddington monsters care nothing for chivalry, so there's no saying how low they'll stoop. They probably won't even apologize as they're killing me.

I was so nervous I couldn't even eat tonight. That will mean I'll be really light-headed when we ride out tomorrow. I might fall off my horse and become our side's first casualty before the battle has even begun.

But I must stay strong for Isolde. Things are going really well with her at the moment. It will really spoil it if I jump down from my horse and run screaming back to my straw as we're setting out tomorrow.

GET REAL

Knights were the most powerful force on the medieval battlefield, but even they could be defeated with good tactics. Groups of knights rode together in a cavalry charge, so foot soldiers would try to cut individual knights off to attack them. They would surround the knights and hold out sharp wooden sticks so their horses couldn't rush at them.

March 29th

We are no longer planning to venture out and attack the Froddington knights. You'd think I'd be pretty relieved, right?

Wrong. The reason we're no longer going out to attack the Froddington knights is because they've returned with over fifty knights from Perilworth Castle and we are now under siege.

Sir Reginald reckons the Froddington knights must have promised the Perilworth lot some of the fingers when they get them back. The idea of dividing the sacred digits has made him even angrier and even more determined to hang on to them.

We've never been under siege before, and I'm sure it will be awful. We could be trapped in here for weeks, starving to death while the surrounding forces grin and wait.

Why did this have to happen while poor Isolde was here? She should never have been dragged into this. Squaring up to your foes on the field of battle is one thing, but cutting off everyone inside a castle is just rude.

I'm starting to think we should just give them the fingers back. We had a good quest, and I got to prove my worth. But it turns out the Froddington lot are taking it far too seriously, and we should just let them have their way.

GET REAL

Castles might have had brilliant defenses, but an attacking army could always use time as a weapon. If they surrounded a castle and cut off its food supplies, they could force the people inside to surrender or starve. If they were feeling especially ruthless, they could even poison the water supply.

March 30ᵗʰ

The enemy knights are obviously planning a
big attack. They're shifting earth into our moat
so they can get nearer to us. Sir Lionel and
Sir Robert ran into the armory and lugged out
a huge wooden pole with a hook on the end.
All day I've been watching them swipe at the
Perilworth and Froddington knights from the
top of the gatehouse. It's like watching a really
weird fishing contest. Every now and then they
get the hook into the armor of a knight, yank
him off his horse, and splat him to the ground.
They're doing their best, but there are just
too many of the enemy knights. They're still
managing to shove earth into our moat.

Chapter II
—
We Go into Battle

March 31st

So that's what they were filling the moat in
for. Today the enemy knights wheeled a huge
wooden tower toward the east side of the castle.
Unlike the scaling ladder, we wouldn't be able
to just push it over. It was really heavy, and
thicker at the bottom than the top.

Sir Reginald called all the knights to the east
tower to prepare for battle. We huddled on the
top and watched through the battlements as
the enemy's massive structure approached.
I drew my sword and held it forward with my
trembling hand.

Their wooden tower stopped a few feet
away from our stone one. Their drawbridge
was lowered down until it rested on our
battlements, and the enemy knights
charged out.

Sir Lionel and Sir Robert rushed at them. They managed to boot the first knight through a gap in the battlements and stab the second in the gap above his breastplate, but more and more knights came out. There were ladders and platforms inside the tower, allowing reinforcements to rush up from the ground.

Soon the small circular roof of the tower was packed with Froddington and Perilworth knights. I took a few steps back and let the others surge past.

The tower was a blur of clacking, glinting blades. Enemy knights were pushed over the battlements, only to be replaced by others. At the front of our pack, Sir Robert stumbled and collapsed.

I didn't like the way this was going. Every time one of their knights was hurt, another emerged from the wooden tower. But every time one of ours went down, there was no one to replace him. Soon I'd be the only one left, and what use would I be against this endless stream of villains? I thought I might as well hurl myself over the edge of the tower right away.

Out of the corner of my eye, I spotted Sir Lionel running down the staircase. I couldn't believe it. I'd thought he was the bravest knight of us all, yet he was proving himself to be a massive coward.

I was about to run away too when I thought about Isolde. If she saw me fleeing danger, I'd never win her heart. I needed to stand my ground in case she was watching.

A few moments later, Sir Lionel returned to the roof carrying a bow and a flaming arrow. He fired the burning arrow over the enemy knights and into their tower.

There were screams of panic from inside as flames spread through the structure. Fire engulfed their drawbridge, and the tower shook violently from side to side.

We pushed forward to attack the knights that remained on the castle. Well, I say "we," but I stood at the back and kept on trembling.

Sir Reginald let out a roar and pushed enemy after enemy through the battlements. The rest were easily overpowered. Soon our heroes were marching them down to the castle dungeons.

I feel sorry for them getting locked up down there. Not because of all the torture devices, but because Gavin will go on and on at them for being terrible prisoners.

I marched at the back of the procession, carrying some of the enemy's swords to our armory. I thought I'd better give myself an important role in case Isolde spotted us.

I'm back on the east tower now, helping to keep lookout as the sky goes dark. There's no sign of the enemy, and the charred remains of their wooden tower are lying in our moat.

No doubt they're plotting their next attack. I just hope they let us get some sleep first. I know I didn't actually do any fighting today, but I still found it really stressful and I'd like to have a rest now.

GET REAL

Siege towers let attackers get over defensive walls with much greater protection than ladders, because of their covered sides. They were large and difficult to move, so they were often constructed on the site of a siege when ladder assaults had failed.

*April I*st

The enemy are still surrounding us, but they
have made no further attempt to attack.

After a while of staring at them from the top
of the tower, I went down to the dungeons to
see Gavin.

There were enemy knights on the rack, the
Judas Chair, the boot, and the thumbscrews,
leaving him with nothing to do but slump in the
corner. Even the rats weren't around to nibble
his feet.

I told him about the siege and he tried to sound
interested, but I could tell he was upset about
missing out on his torture.

But when I mentioned that I had to go back
up to the towers to check if the enemies were

returning, he really perked up. He said he'd assumed the siege was over.

He got excited when he realized it was still going on, and he started telling me about all the sieges he'd been in before and how he'd nearly starved to death. He said hunger is worse than every other type of torture combined when it goes on for long enough, and he couldn't wait for it to happen again.

It's alright for him. He loves agony. But we'll all have to go through it if the siege continues for ages. I really hope things get sorted out soon.

April 2nd

The siege is over. Or so they want us to think.

There was no sign of the enemy this morning. According to the guards, they'd disappeared during a storm in the night.

I know it's a trick. They'll be hiding in the woods to the east or west of the castle, or in the hills behind us. No doubt they want us to venture out so they can massacre us.

I asked Sir Lionel what he thought I should do, and he said I should leave the castle.

I made it clear I wasn't volunteering to track the enemy and wipe them out single-handedly, but that wasn't what he had in mind.

He handed me a large wooden bowl and told me to fill it with water and walk around the castle, placing it on the ground. If I found a spot that made the water ripple, I should hold my hand up to let him know.

He said he'd get the guards to keep an eye on me from the castle walls and raise flags if there was any sign of the enemy, so I wouldn't be in any danger. And if what he suspected were true, we wouldn't see any sign of the enemy today anyway.

I couldn't turn him down, especially as this quest sounded much easier than most, but I was still very nervous. Even if the guards managed to give me a lot of warning, the enemy hoards might pounce before I could make it back.

I grabbed a wooden bowl from the kitchens and filled it with water from the well. I was about

to pop outside, but then I remembered I was
meant to dedicate all my quests to Isolde now.

I found Isolde in the great hall, talking to
Thomas. I told her I was about to perform a
brave deed for her. She seemed disappointed to
find all it involved was walking around with a
bowl of water. But I reckoned I could still get
killed doing it, so she should at least know I did
it in her name.

175

After that, I strode outside and placed the bowl of water on the ground. There were definitely ripples. That settled it, then. I couldn't believe I'd completed my task straight away.

But then I took my hand away and the ripples stopped. It was just my trembling hand that had been causing them.

I ventured a few feet farther out and tried again. Still nothing. After a while I spotted all the other knights gathering to watch me on the wall. I really hoped Sir Lionel wasn't just using me as bait to get the enemy knights out of their hiding place.

With everyone looking, I had to prove myself. I ventured farther and farther out to find the ripples.

Eventually I got a result. Over toward the west forest, I put the bowl on the ground and tiny ripples spread across the surface. I stepped away, just to make sure I wasn't causing them.

They were still there. I turned to the roof and raised my hand.

Sir Reginald and Sir Robert came charging out of the gatehouse. They were armed not with swords but with shovels.

I stood and watched as they dug huge clumps of earth out of the ground and tossed them over their shoulders. Soon there was a deep hole where the bowl had been.

Sir Lionel emerged from the castle too, carrying a flaming torch and a pile of straw.

He peered into the tunnel and smiled. I looked down and saw the terrified face of a man staring up at us. Sir Reginald waved at him, and Sir Lionel set fire to a handful of the straw and dropped it down.

There were cries of panic from far below us, followed by the sound of scurrying feet.

April 3rd

Everyone has been congratulating me on my daring mission, even though I didn't have a clue why I was doing it at the time. It turns out Sir Lionel was using an old trick to check for tunnels. The ripples were caused by the enemy digging in the soil far below us.

Isolde thanked me for dedicating the heroic deed to her when I saw her in the hall. I'm glad the mission turned out to be a genuinely important one. It wouldn't have looked great if it had just been a way to get rid of me for a few hours.

Now that their tunnel plan has failed, the enemy knights have returned to surround us. So we're back under siege and back to worrying about starving to death. But at least they didn't tunnel into our courtyard and stab us while we slept.

*April 4*th

The enemy have stepped up their attack. This morning I was woken by a huge crash. I ran to the top of the west tower to see the enemy knights firing huge rocks at us with a giant wooden machine.

There was a large crowd of squires and castle staff watching as the enemy reloaded the machine. Some of them were sobbing with fear.

A rock thudded into the wall below us, and I leaned forward to see hundreds of tiny stone flakes crumble to the ground.

Sir Lionel appeared and ordered everyone except the knights and guards into the keep. Geoffrey and Thomas looked really annoyed as they slouched past me. I told them us knights would protect them, which just made them even angrier.

As soon as they'd gone, a massive rock whizzed past my ears and I wished I'd been allowed to join them. I peered over the battlements and watched the enemies readying their weapon to use again. I was quaking so much my armor started to rattle.

GET REAL

A trebuchet was a siege weapon that could hurl heavy objects such as rocks. The objects were placed in a sling on the end of a long wooden arm that was set in motion by a falling weight. As well as stones, the trebuchet was used to fling rotting meat, sharp sticks, and dung.

April 5ᵗʰ

We can't take much more of this. The enemy knights kept on bombarding us all night. Most of our walls were too strong for their rocks, but this morning they smashed a hole in one of the rear towers. Sooner or later they're going to smash through and swarm in.

This afternoon the regular crashes were interrupted by a splat. Instead of another rock, they'd thrown the back half of a dead cow into our courtyard. According to Sir Lionel, they're trying to spread diseases by flinging rotten meat. Sir Hugh lugged the stinky carcass up to the top of the east tower and tossed it into the ditch.

I really think we should just hand over Saint Stephen's fingers now. I know it's not very brave or noble to give in, but the enemy totally outnumber us, they've got terrifying weapons, and they're totally ruthless.

The Yellowfriars monks have still got plenty of relics to be getting on with. Let's just cut our losses and let the Froddington and Perilworth knights have the fingers.

Chapter 12
—
An Unexpected Discovery

April 6ᵗʰ

We were standing on the east tower and watching the enemy pelt us with rocks this afternoon when Brother Fendrel ran into the courtyard and announced he had grave news.

We followed him back to the chapel, ducking the falling rocks.

Brother Fendrel pointed at the altar, where long grey shapes had been lined up next to a small cloth sack. It took me a moment to recognize them as Saint Stephen's fingers.

The monk said he'd decided to examine the holy relic to pass the time during the siege.

He pointed to the fingers and asked us if we noticed anything strange about them. No one said anything, so I pointed out that they were much greyer and more shriveled than normal ones.

That wasn't what he was getting at. The odd thing he had actually spotted was that there were fourteen fingers and three thumbs.

Sir Reginald threw himself to the floor and declared it a miracle that Saint Stephen had been given so many fingers and thumbs.

Brother Fendrel shook his head. Apparently, there was no mention in any of the records of Saint Stephen having freakishly massive hands with loads of fingers. He said the whole relic must have been fake, and now that he came to think of it, the man they bought it from did look a bit dodgy.

I couldn't believe we'd gone to all the effort of traveling to Froddington, tricking them into handing over the fingers, coming home, and surviving a massive siege for a fake relic.

There was a moment of uncomfortable silence, but then Sir Reginald declared that the fake fingers had been sent to test us and the real ones would be beamed down from heaven if we all stayed in the chapel staring at them for long enough.

Luckily, Sir Lionel had a much better idea.

He said he'd give the worthless relics to the enemy knights to make them go away. Then we'd tell everyone in our castle that the enemy had surrendered and Brother Fendrel had taken the relic back to Yellowfriars.

It might not be very chivalrous and honest to lie, but it would be better than admitting we put everyone through all that stress for nothing.

April 7ᵗʰ

The leaders of the Froddington and Perilworth knights accepted the relic and have now gone. As far as they're concerned, they've been victorious and won their holy relic back. Little do they know the crusty digits were probably dug up from some plague pit and have been no nearer to Saint Stephen than my fingers have.

Our enemies didn't want to divide the fingers, so the Froddington lot will get custody of them in the summer and the Perilworth knights will get them in the winter. Sir Lionel reckons this isn't going to work and they'll be at war with each other over the fingers soon. That's fine by me. As long as they don't pelt us with rocks and cows, I don't mind what they do.

Sir Reginald has gone back to Yellowfriars Monastery with Brother Fendrel now. I think he's a little annoyed with us for giving up the relic so easily, even though it wasn't genuine. I'm sure he'll feel fine again once he's spent a few days with the other relics in the monastery. I know how much he enjoys looking at Saint Paul's earlobe.

Chapter 13
—
A New
Quest

April 8th

We're having a massive feast to celebrate our victory in a couple of days, but I won't enjoy it as much as the last one. I know we have to go ahead with it to keep up appearances, but I don't feel very victorious this time.

Looking on the bright side, it will give me another chance to talk to Isolde. I could even dedicate my role in the glorious victory to her, and I bet she'll be really impressed.

I spotted Leofric slumped in the corner of the courtyard this afternoon. He said he was trying to write some material for the feast, but he was struggling.

He has no one to try out his material on now that I'm busy with knight stuff, no one ever laughs anyway, and he's considering packing it in and becoming a juggler.

I wanted to tell him he'd get better at the comedy if he stuck with it, but I didn't feel in much of a mood to reassure him. I told him I didn't think I was a very good knight either. I was still feeling guilty about pretending we'd beaten the Froddington and Perilworth knights, but I couldn't say anything. We've all promised to keep it secret.

For once, it was Leofric who reassured me. He said he thought things had been going brilliantly for me, and loads of people in the castle had been talking about how well I've been doing.

It gave me a real boost in confidence to find out people think of me that way. Maybe I haven't been doing too badly after all.

WORLD'S WORST KNIGHT

April 9ᵗʰ

I went down to the dungeons to see Gavin today. I thought he'd be much happier now that the other prisoners have gone, but he still seemed glum.

I asked him what was wrong, and he said he was bored with all our torture equipment. Even the Judas Chair loses its power when you've been on it a million times.

I told him I'd put a word in with Sir Lionel and see if he'd buy something new. I don't think it's likely, though. He'll have to spend loads of money repairing the trebuchet damage and won't have anything left over for fancy torture stuff.

Then I had a brilliant idea. A few minutes later I was back in the dungeons, and I had Leofric with me.

I don't know why I didn't think of it sooner. Leofric will get to try out his new material, and Gavin will get to experience a totally new type of torture.

As I went back upstairs again, I could hear Leofric going through some one-liners and Gavin wincing with agony.

It felt great to have helped.

April 10th

The feast has been canceled!

Sir Reginald came back from Yellowfriars with shocking news. The toenails of Saint Edmund have been stolen from Coddington Monastery in the far north of the country.

He's vowed that we'll travel there, track down the toenails and return them.

All the other knights thought this was a great idea, so I agreed. It will be much tougher this time. We'll have to travel hundreds of miles before we can even start searching for the toenails.

But at least we know we're hunting for a top-quality relic. Everyone's heard of the toenails of Saint Edmund. Even if someone could name only five relics, they'd be on the list.

As the others scrambled to get ready, I tracked down Isolde. She was sitting in the courtyard with Thomas, and I had to interrupt their conversation to dedicate my quest to her.

She looked really impressed and said she hoped I'd do well.

I think I will. My life as a knight hasn't got off to a very smooth start, but I'm sure I'll get the hang of it soon.

I've got a good feeling about this quest. I reckon that by the end of it, I'll be the sort of brave, noble, chivalrous hero I've always wanted to be.

The End

Knights and Castles

Roderick's diary was written in the early 14th century, in a period we call the "Middle Ages." This is because it came between the great classical age of Greece and Rome, and the Renaissance, when interest in the classical era was revived.

These centuries were once dismissed as a dark and mysterious era when progress and learning were on hold. But we now see them as a rich and fascinating time.

One of the most famous figures from the Middle Ages is the knight. Knights were soldiers who wore armor and rode on horseback. Some fought for lords and kings, while others fought for themselves.

At first, knights wore chain mail made from small iron rings. But this soon developed into full suits of plate armor.

Knights featured in many of the myths and other literature of the era. Stories of loyal, fair, and brave knights were popular, and many of these survive to this day. For example, the stories of King Arthur and the Knights of the Round Table have inspired countless modern books, films, and TV shows.

But it wasn't enough for knights to be brave and loyal. They had to be sentimental too. Many stories of knights portrayed them as love-struck warriors, proving their love for noble women by going on difficult quests.

Just as famous as the courageous knights are the grand castles they lived in, many of which are still standing today.

At first, castles were wooden buildings surrounded by fences and ditches. A motte-and-bailey castle had a tower built on a mound of earth (a motte) and a courtyard lower down (a bailey).

Wooden castles were eventually replaced by stone ones. Although these took longer to build, they were much harder to attack. They soon developed into awesome structures with towers, winding staircases, dungeons, great halls, and gatehouses.

The spread of gunpowder from the
15th century onward signaled the end of the
era of knights and castles. But the romantic
idea of the armored warrior on horseback
lived on.

Knights still exist in the modern world, but
the title is given as a reward for services
rendered to a country. So while Bill Gates,
George H.W. Bush, and Sir Elton John are
knights, don't expect them to set out on
horseback to rescue you if you're in trouble.

How do we know about the Middle Ages?

One of the reasons the Middle Ages were sometimes called the "Dark Ages" was because fewer written records survive than from other periods. But there are still plenty of sources that show us what medieval life was like.

There are records of events, such as the Anglo-Saxon Chronicle, which was written by monks.

There are legal documents, such as the Magna Carta, which was signed by King John in 1215. This famous charter limited his control over English barons.

There are the personal letters people sent, which often include details of everyday life that were left out of official documents.

There are works of literature, such as *The Canterbury Tales* by Geoffrey Chaucer. This is a collection of stories told by characters on a pilgrimage to Canterbury.

One very important document from the Middle Ages is the *Domesday Book*. This is a survey of England and parts of Wales ordered in 1086 by William the Conqueror. It lists details such as how many people lived in each village and who owned the land.

Besides written records, we can also learn about medieval life by examining works of art that have survived. And we can visit the many buildings that still stand, such as castles.

Timeline

1066

Norman knights from France invade Britain, and William the Conqueror takes the throne.

1095

The start of the Crusades. These were holy wars fought between Christians and Muslims, and many knights took part.

1118

A military order known as the Knights Templar is formed to help Christian pilgrims in the Holy Land.

1215

The Magna Carta is signed by King John.

1264

Simon de Montfort leads a revolt against King Henry III and briefly rules over England. He's killed the following year by forces loyal to the king.

Timeline

1291

The Crusades end as the last Christian stronghold is taken by a Muslim army.

1337

The start of the Hundred Years' War between England and France.

1349

An outbreak of bubonic plague known as the Black Death kills tens of millions.

1381

An army of peasants marches on London to protest against things such as high rents and the poll tax. The uprising became known as the Peasants' Revolt.

1415

The Battle of Agincourt takes place, ending in a famous victory for the English over the French.

1453

The Hundred Years' War ends, sixteen years later than you might expect.

1455

The Wars of the Roses start, a series of battles for the throne of England fought between the houses of Lancaster and York.

1485

Henry VII wins the Battle of Bosworth Field, ending the Wars of the Roses. The Tudor era begins.

1492

Christopher Columbus crosses the Atlantic and lands on islands in the Caribbean. His voyage to what became known as the New World would change the course of history.

Knight Hall of Fame

William the Conqueror (c.1027-1087)

William of Normandy invaded England in 1066. He became king after defeating Harold at the Battle of Hastings and reigned until his death in 1087.

El Cid (c.1043-1099)

Rodrigo Diaz de Vivar, nicknamed El Cid, meaning "the lord," was a Spanish knight famed for his battle tactics.

Thomas Beckett (1118-1170)

Thomas Beckett was the Archbishop of Canterbury in the reign of King Henry II. He was murdered by the king's knights in Canterbury Cathedral.

Saladin (c.1137-1193)

Saladin was the Sultan of Egypt who reclaimed Jerusalem from Christian crusaders. He is remembered as one of the great Muslim leaders.

Knight Hall of Fame

Richard I (1157-1199)

Richard I was an English king known as "Richard the Lionheart." He spent much of his reign fighting abroad. He defended lands in France and fought with crusaders in the Holy Land.

King John (1167-1216)

The younger brother of Richard the Lionheart, King John is remembered for signing the Magna Carta. He is often depicted as a villain in stories about Robin Hood.

Simon de Montfort (c.1208-1265)

Simon de Montfort was the Earl of Leicester. He led a revolt against King Henry III.

Geoffrey Chaucer (c.1340-1400)

Geoffrey Chaucer was the most famous author of the Middle Ages. He wrote *The Canterbury Tales*.

212

Knight Hall of Fame

Wat Tyler (Died 1381)

Wat Tyler led the English Peasants' Revolt of 1381. He was killed by the Lord Mayor of London, William Walworth, during the battle.

Henry V (c.1387-1422)

Henry V was the English king who defeated the French at the battle of Agincourt.

Johannes Gutenberg (c.1398-1468)

Johannes Gutenberg was a German inventor who developed a method of printing using moveable metal type. His method increased the speed at which books could be made, allowing for the rapid spread of knowledge.

Joan of Arc (c.1412-1431)

Joan of Arc was a French peasant who led French forces against the English. She was burned at the stake in Rouen in 1431 but became an even bigger heroine to the French after her death.

Glossary

Battlement
A design seen on the top of castle walls, with gaps for firing arrows. The gaps were called crenels.

Bloodletting
A medical treatment in which patients were deliberately made to lose blood. It was based on the mistaken belief that illness was caused by too much blood.

Chamber Pot
A bowl-shaped container used as a toilet. It was the job of servants to empty them.

Chivalry
The code of conduct knights followed, encouraging bravery, honor, and loyalty.

Coat-of-arms
The symbols on the shield or robe that identify a knight. A coat-of-arms helped knights tell friends from enemies in battle.

Crusades
A series of holy wars between Christians and Muslims, beginning in 1095 and ending in 1291.

Dubbing A ceremony in which a squire was made into a knight.

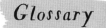
Glossary

Feudal System
The division of medieval society into kings, noblemen, knights, and peasants.

Greave
A piece of armor used to protect the shin.

Jester
An entertainer who performed jokes as well as music, storytelling, and acrobatics.

Joust
Staged combat between two knights on horseback with lances.

Keep
A large stone tower built within the walls of a castle. It could sometimes be defended as a last resort if enemies broke through the castle walls.

Lance
A pole weapon used by soldiers on horseback. Lances often had a wooden shaft and a pointed steel end.

Medieval / The Middle Ages
The period of history between the 5th century and the 15th century.

Glossary

Peasants
The people at the bottom of the feudal system. They worked hard to farm the land owned by a lord.

Portcullis
A metal gate that could be lowered to block the entrance to a castle and defend against enemies.

Quintain
An object such as a shield mounted on a post, used as a target in jousting exercises.

Siege
Surrounding a castle and cutting it off from supplies to make the people inside surrender.

Spinning Wheel
A device for spinning things such as wool and flax into yarn or thread. It had a spindle driven by a large wheel.

Squire
A young man, typically between the ages of 14 and 21, who was training to become a knight.

Trebuchet
A large wooden weapon used in sieges to hurl large stones and dead animals into castles.